Happy Ever After

For Cerys
S.W.

ORCHARD BOOKS
338 Euston Road, London NW1 3BH
Orchard Books Australia
Hachette Children's Books
Level 17/207, Kent Street, Sydney, NSW 2000
ISBN 1 84362 523 7 (hardback)
ISBN 1 84362 531 8 (paperback)
First published in Great Britain in 2005
First paperback publication in 2006
Text © Tony Bradman 2005 Illustrations © Sarah Warburton 2005
The rights of Tony Bradman to be identified as the author
and of Sarah Warburton to be identified as the illustrator of this
work have been asserted by them in accordance with the Copyright,
Designs and Patents Act, 1988. A CIP catalogue record for this book is
available from the British Library.
1 3 5 7 9 10 8 6 4 2 (hardback)
1 3 5 7 9 10 8 6 4 2 (paperback)
The text paper this book is printed on is certified by the Forest
Stewardship Council (FSC). FSC products with percentage claims
meet environmental requirements to be ancient-forest friendly.
The printer Cox & Wyman holds FSC chain of custody TT-COC-2063.
Printed in Great Britain by Cox & Wyman, CPI Group.

FSC
Mixed Sources
Product group from well-managed
forests and other controlled sources
Cert no. TT-COC-2063
www.fsc.org
© 1996 Forest Stewardship Council

Tony Bradman

Happy Ever After

MR WOLF
BOUNCES BACK

Illustrated by Sarah Warburton

ORCHARD BOOKS

Night was falling, and deep in the heart
of the forest the shadows were gathering
round Mr Wolf as he trailed down the
path towards home.

It had been a very bad day. For one thing, Mr Wolf had failed to catch any of the Three Little Pigs. It was odd, he thought - he could easily have snapped up the first two, yet for some reason he'd let them get away.

And though he'd huffed and puffed at
the third little pig's house, his heart
hadn't really been in it.

As for that disaster with Little Red Riding Hood - it had all been going so well, too. He had been quite enjoying pretending to be her granny, and the "what-big-eyes-and-teeth-you've-got" game.

Then, suddenly, that nasty woodcutter had burst into the cottage and gone for him with an axe.

"Oh no!" said Mrs Wolf when Mr Wolf got home. "Are you all right, dear? What happened this time?"

"It's a long story," said Mr Wolf, sitting down. "Actually, it's two long stories, but I'll tell you later. Where are the cubs?"

"Daddy!" squeaked three bundles of grey fur. They raced up to him and jumped onto his lap. He couldn't help smiling, even though he was worn out. "What's for dinner, Daddy?" they squeaked.

"I'm sorry, kids," said Mr Wolf. "I was hoping we'd be having roast little pig this evening, but I, er...had a few problems..."

"Not to worry," said Mrs Wolf cheerily. "Too much meat probably isn't good for us. I'll soon rustle something else up."

And that's what she did. The supper she made was very tasty. Afterwards, Mr Wolf played rough and tumble with the cubs...

And at bedtime he read them their favourite stories.

Once they were asleep, he made a nice pot of tea, and sat by the fire with Mrs Wolf. "I used to be brilliant at bringing home the bacon," he muttered. "But these days I'm just hopeless."

He couldn't understand it. He'd always been known in the forest as the Big Bad Wolf - the strongest, fastest and scariest wolf of them all. So why couldn't he catch anything for his family to eat?

Suddenly, he realised what the problem was – he couldn't hurt little creatures any more. These days they all reminded him of his own cubs...

"Right, that's it," Mr Wolf said at last.
"I've come to a decision."

"Really?" said Mrs Wolf. "What are
you going to do?"

"I'll get a different job," said Mr Wolf.
"That's what!"

So, the next morning, Mr Wolf rose early, and washed and combed his fur.

He waved goodbye to Mrs Wolf and dropped the cubs off at school.

Then he headed for the Forest Job Centre. He took a deep breath and went in.

He sat in the waiting room. Then he
was shown into the office of Mrs Bear.

"Hello," she said, smiling. "How may I
help you today?"

"I'd like a job," Mr Wolf said nervously.
"Er...please."

"OK, just fill out this form for me..." said Mrs Bear. "You don't have many qualifications, do you? Apart from being strong, fast and scary, that is. What kind of a job did you have in mind?"

KNOW
YOUR
RIGHTS

"Actually, I think I need a complete career change," said Mr Wolf.

"Terrific!" said Mrs Bear, peering at her computer. "I like a challenge. Ah, here we are - this one is very different..."

Mrs Bear sent him to the Forest China Shop - and the manager gave him the job. But the shop was full of delicate plates, bowls and cups...

Mr Wolf didn't know his own strength, so he kept breaking things when he picked them up. He did a lot of damage with his tail, too.

He was back at the Forest Job Centre long before lunchtime.

"Not to worry," said Mrs Bear. "Umm, now let me see... You enjoy running around in the open air, don't you? Try this one..."

The next day, Mr Wolf went to the Forest Post Office, where they gave him a job delivering the post. "This is more like it!" he thought.

But he raced round his route so fast that he upset the other postmen. They couldn't compete, and said he was a show-off.

Mr Wolf trailed back to Mrs Bear, his tail tucked between his legs.

"You're turning out to be more of a challenge than I thought," said Mrs Bear. "But I'm not giving up. Try this one."

So, the next morning, Mr Wolf went to the palace, where he was given a job as a royal servant.

He was more nervous than ever now, but he was determined to do his best. And things didn't go too badly to begin with.

Later that day, there was a royal banquet, and Mr Wolf was almost run off his paws. Some of the guests weren't very nice - in fact, the Ugly Sisters and the Wicked Stepmother were so rude that he finally lost his temper.

This time, Mr Wolf didn't wait to
be sacked. He went straight home to
his family.

That evening, Mr Wolf looked down at his lovely cubs as they lay sleeping. He was really worried now. He wasn't making any money, or bringing home any food, and soon the cupboard would be completely bare...

At the Forest Job Centre the next day, Mrs Bear was looking grim.

"*Too* strong... *too* fast... *too* scary," she said.

"I'm sorry, but I'll have to admit defeat - I can't find you a job. Why don't you go back to what you used to do? Now if you don't mind, I've got another appointment..."

Mr Wolf left her office and stood in the shadows of the corridor. He was so miserable he barely noticed the couple going into Mrs Bear's office.

Then he heard something through the door that caught his attention, and he crept over to listen.

"We're really worried about our little ones," somebody was saying.

"I'm really worried about mine too," thought Mr Wolf. He sneaked a peek round the door, and saw that it was Mr Pig talking.

"We still think of them as little even though they have left home."

"Last week was awful," said Mrs Pig. "It made us think it might be a good idea to hire somebody to keep an eye on them."

"What, like a sort of...security guard?"
said Mrs Bear.

"I suppose so," said Mr Pig. "Someone
who knows all the tricks wolves get up
to, and who's strong, fast and scary
enough to see them off."

"Goodness, what a coincidence!" said
Mrs Bear. "It would be the perfect job
for somebody who was in earlier today.
I'll send him round to you."

Mr Wolf smiled. Maybe there was hope, after all. When Mr and Mrs Pig left, he stepped out of the shadows and slipped into Mrs Bear's office...

Mrs Bear did send him to see Mr and Mrs Pig. Of course, Mr Wolf had to disguise himself to get the job. Mr and Mrs Pig would never have hired the Big Bad Wolf. But a wolf in sheep's clothing - well, that was a different matter.

Mr Wolf soon proved just how good he was at his new job, too. On his very first day he caught a young wolf trying to climb into the brick house through a half-open window.

Mr Wolf pounced swiftly, and grabbed the intruder from behind. "Oh no you don't, my lad," he growled in his scariest voice, and sent the terrified young wolf packing.

Mr Wolf loved his job. He loved
playing with the Three Little Pigs, and
reading them stories.

He had no trouble keeping his paws off them, either - Mrs Wolf had decided the Wolf family should go vegetarian. And now they had plenty of money to buy the food they needed. The Wolf cubs thrived.

And so, much to his surprise, Mr Wolf really did live...

HAPPILY EVER AFTER!

Happy Ever After

Written by Tony Bradman

Illustrated by Sarah Warburton

These books are available from all good bookshops, or can be ordered direct
from the publisher: Orchard Books, PO BOX 29, Douglas IM99 1BQ.
Credit card orders please telephone 01624 836000 or fax 01624 837033 or
visit our Internet site: www.wattspub.co.uk or
e-mail: bookshop@enterprise.net for details.

To order please quote title, author and ISBN and your full name and
address. Cheques and postal orders should be made payable to 'Bookpost
plc.' Postage and packing is FREE within the UK
(overseas customers should add £1.00 per book).

Prices and availability are subject to change.